British Library Cataloguing in Publication Data
McKee, David
  Two can toucan.
  I. Title
  823'.914(J)   PZ7

  ISBN 0-86264-094-6

Text © 1964 by David McKee.
Illustrations © 1985 by David McKee.
First published in Great Britain in 1985 by Andersen Press Ltd., 20 Vauxhall Bridge Road,
London SW1V 2SA. Published in Australia by Random House Australia Pty. Ltd.,
20 Alfred Street, Milsons Point, Sydney NSW 2061. All rights reserved.
Colour separated by Photolitho AG Offsetreproduktionen, Gossau, Zürich, Switzerland.
Printed and bound in Italy by Grafiche AZ, Verona.

3 4 5 6 7 8 9

TWO CAN TOUCAN

David McKee

Andersen Press London

There was once a bird who didn't have a name. He had a very large beak and was all black except for the whites of his eyes.

All the other creatures, who had names, laughed at him. This made him very unhappy.

One day he decided to leave them all and go to seek his fortune.

He went over the mountain . . .

Then across the river . . .

Until he came to a hot dusty place where everybody worked.
This made him want to work as well.

So he went to see a man, sitting behind a large desk, who told him what to try.

At first he tried chopping wood, but his beak was so large that it always got in the way.

Next he tried office work, but he felt silly in a bowler hat.

Finally he tried carrying things. He enjoyed doing this and was very good at it.

Most of the time he carried cans. Because of his long beak he could carry two at once.

The others called him "Two Can" as they could only carry one. He was happy, at last he had a name.

One day when Two Can was carrying paint, instead of being content with two he tried to carry three cans.

Going down some steps, he fell and ended up with orange, red and white paint all over him.

Although he scrubbed and scrubbed, he could not get the paint off.

He felt he was a failure, and one morning, before the city was awake, he left for home.

He went back across the river . . .

Then back over the mountain . . .

When at last he arrived home none of the creatures
recognized him in his fine new feathers.

When they asked his name, he said it was "Two Can".

They spelled it T-O-U-C-A-N so he decided to keep it that way.

Toucan explained who he was and told them about his adventures. When they heard the story they all laughed again.

But this time Toucan laughed with them!